DISCARDED

SCRiBBLE WiTCH

DISCARDED

Magical Muddles

Spellings and doodlings
by Inky Willis

Dedicated to... Bodiam Class 2020

CHAPTER ONE

This is me, **Molly Mills,** and this is my school:

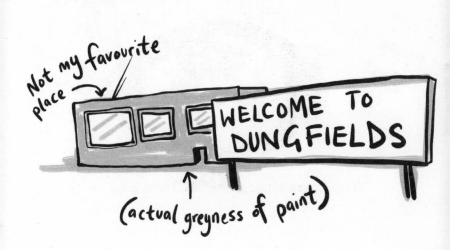

Not my favourite place →

WELCOME TO DUNGFIELDS

↑ (actual greyness of paint)

My best friend, Chloe, used to go to Dungfields too, but now she goes to Lady Juniper's School for Girls.

Chloe ↙

From what she's told me Lady Juniper's looks more or less like this:

Angels playing harps in East wing →

permanent rainbow ↑

When Chloe changed schools, I was a bit upset.

I may have been a bit over the top.

But, actually, it's not so bad.

I mean, yeah, it's *bad*. We've been besties
since for ever. Since before we even knew what
besties were. So I'm not exactly the laughing
queen of Happyland now she's gone.

nope

BUT it would have been SO much worse if it wasn't for Notes.

Notes is the paper scribble witch who lives in my pen pot. She's magic (of course) and my friend (hooray!) and she's a total **HERO!**

Here's my top ten things you absolutely have to know about my friend Notes:

10. Notes likes helping (this doesn't always go to plan but she tries REALLY hard!).

9. Notes talks kind of funny. Actually, she doesn't talk at all, she just writes notes (super fast). But she writes kind of funny. You'll see.

8. Notes is secret. Only ~~friendlings~~ friends can see Notes. This is because she's made of paper and doesn't want to be crumpled up by mean people.

7. Notes is scribbly. She's literally a scribble.

6. Notes was drawn by a sad kid (mystery!) and I found her and cut her out when I was sad too. And cutting her out was like some kind of magic spell, because suddenly she was alive!!

5. Notes has a pencil topper that's also a (tiny) real cat. I don't totally get how that works. His name is Captain Purrkins.

4. Notes sleeps in the pen pot on my desk. She curls round the inside so she doesn't get crumpled by pencils.

3. Notes has a magic flying pencil instead of a broomstick. She can write magic notes with it and her friends can read them.

2. Notes flies my notes all the way to Chloe, and flies Chloe's notes all the way back to me (see — hero!).

1. Notes eats pencil shavings. That's not something I love about her particularly (I'm fine with it, though) — it's just a fact.

So, yeah, the first few days without Chloe were hard. But with my hero (Notes) to help me I was doing OK ... right up until I got this:

Hi Molly!

Don't worry about me! There aren't many kids in my class, which is weird, but I've made some amazing friends. There's Eliza — she's got a cinema room at her house. There's Deena — she's an actual genius. And I told you about Daffodil, right? She tells these jokes that make you laugh even though they're not funny. She reminds me of you a bit. So I'm totally completely fine.

Chloe x

P.S. All my friends have signed up for the Inter-School Spelling Championship and guess who's agreed to do it too? Me!!!

I know, right?!

It was break time when Notes delivered that message from Chloe. I'd been hanging out on my own, hiding in the Secret Spot (which is basically just a hollow bush at the end of the field). I was really hoping a letter would arrive, and – **whoop!** – along came Notes and Captain Purrkins, riding on a paper plane.

And I was SO excited when I started reading!
I felt like a bouncy castle all puffed up with *glee*.
But then I read the letter and all the glee hissed
out of me.

BEFORE   AFTER

For a long while I just sat there, frowning
at the piece of paper. Notes even flew up to
my forehead at one point and tried to push the
creases apart. Captain Purrkins pushed his tiny

head against my neck, trying (I hope!) to comfort me.

I had two huge problems with Chloe's letter.

Firstly, this INTER-WHATSIT SPELLING THING. Chloe used to hate spelling tests. I hate spelling tests. Hating spelling tests was our *thing*. It was a huge part of our friendship. Who was this new Chloe with her **why not give it a go** attitude?

Secondly, and maybe I was being selfish, but isn't settling in and making new friends supposed to take a while?

Did she miss me even a teeny bit?

I mean, how could she miss me when she had all those exciting new friends? How could I compete with cinema rooms and geniuses and girls called Daffodil? Though, for the record, Daffodil is nothing like me because my jokes actually *are* funny.

I mean, I totally did want Chloe to have new friends. I totally DIDN'T want her to be hiding in a bush every break time, waiting for notes from me. But a little I miss you would have been nice.

Notes looked really worried, which then made me feel **MEGA-GUiLTy**. She'd gone to all that trouble flying Chloe's letter to me. I should've been all grins and glee, but I just wasn't feeling it.

So I wasn't surprised when Notes grabbed a leaf and wrote with her magic pencil ...

"I'm fine," I said.

She shook her little head then flipped over the leaf ...

"I'm fine," I said again.

Frowning, she yanked up a blade of grass.

"Really, *really,* really," I sighed.

I looked down at the letter, hoping Notes wouldn't see how **REALLY-NOT-FINE** I was. My heart sank at the thought of writing back to Chloe. She'd be expecting a reply. But I didn't know what to say. There's nothing FLASHY about Dungfields. Nothing impressive. I thought about telling her that we'd got new picnic tables for lunchtime. But then I thought what if everyone at Lady Juniper's eats at restaurant tables with flowers and frilly tablecloths and fancy napkins?!

So I didn't write back right away. Instead I flopped around the Secret Spot, watching

Captain Purrkins bop unlucky flies.

Then, with a sad heart (and dead flies on my jumper), I slunk inside.

CHAPTER TWO

By the time I got back to class I was in a right old funk. A **funk** (in case you're wondering) is a gloomy mood. And this was a **FULL-FROWN SLUMPY-SHOULDERED** kind of funk. The kind of funk no one can help you with (especially not Emily).

Emily sits next to me. She's OK, but she doesn't handle my funks very well. I think they make her uncomfortable.

frown × slump = FUNK!!!

15

When I sat down, she said, "Are you going to do that thing where you huff and sigh and grunt all the way through Maths?"

I said, "Hmph."

Then she mumbled, "Oh, lucky me," and started arranging her stationery. Emily loves stationery just as much as *I* love stationery. The difference is mine's always jumbled up in my pencil case, but Emily likes hers to look ... well ... Emily-ish!

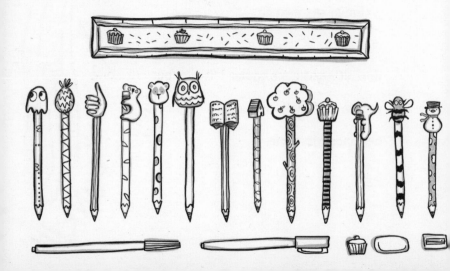

I looked at the empty chair the other side of me where Chloe used to sit. It was **three weeks and two days** since Chloe had left (not that I was counting) and no one had taken her place.

I thought back to her letter about Eliza and Deena and Daffodil.

Perhaps someone totally new would start at
Dungfields. Someone **SUPER SASSY**
called, hmmm **... Bluebell?** Or **Buttercup?** Or
maybe a name that sounded a bit less like a cow.
I know, I thought

The point is, if Chloe had replaced me, then

fine. I wouldn't get all jealous. Nope, not me. I would just stay cool and wait for my new best friend to arrive.

But just as I was wondering what Saffire would look like, my super sarcastic teacher Mr Stilton **coughed.** Mr Stilton is so sarcastic that even his **coughs** sound kind of fake.

"Hack-hem?" he said, going up at the end like he was asking a question.

I thought about answering in cough language too.

"Hackety-hem-hem!"

(But I didn't because then all the super sarcasm would've been aimed at me.)

Mr Stilton was standing at the front of the class, holding a giant dice, ready to do what he calls "the input", which always makes me think of some weird machine with beeps and flashing buttons.

But, actually, it's nowhere near that exciting.

(FACT: one dice isn't called a dice; it's called a die. That's right, a die!

No one says that, though, because it's weird.)

"Eyes this way!" he said. "Who remembers what we've been looking at this week?"

Everyone (probably) remembered, but only Emily put her hand up.

"Probability," said Emily.

"Thank you," said Mr Stilton, glaring at the rest of us.

"So," he said, "if I roll this dice, what's the probability of me getting a six? Tell the person next to you."

The class filled up with mathsy murmurs.

Emily looked crazy-keen to tell me the answer. I really wasn't in the mood for this.

She leaned in towards me like she was worried someone might steal her answer. *"One in six,"* she whispered.

"Urgh," I said.

Emily glared at me and I remembered what she said about me grunting etc. Maybe she had a point.

"Hands up then! Who thinks they know?" said Mr Stilton.

22

Emily's hand instantly shot up, but Mr Stilton was looking the other way.

"Mustafa?"

"One in six?" said Mustafa.

"Who agrees?" said Stilton.

I hate it when he asks who agrees. Because if you <u>DO</u> put your hand up you might get asked why, and if you <u>DON'T</u> put your hand up you might be asked what <u>YOU</u> think the answer is. There is literally <u>no safe option.</u>

I decided to copy everyone else and stuck

my hand in the air. But on its way up my hand accidentally knocked Emily's pencils out of their very, very, VERY

neat row.

She glared at me again and I tried to tell her sorry with my face without actually saying it

(so I wouldn't get told off for talking).

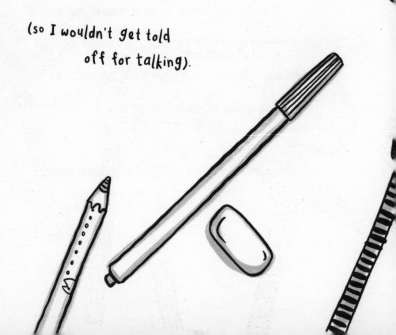

my sorry face

Emily ignored my sorry face and started faffing with her pencils.

"Well done, everyone. All in agreement. Good. Oh — all except for Emily. Emily, please get Molly to explain the answer to you."

Emily's mouth fell open in **HORROR**. Then she snapped it shut and glared at me AGAIN (even though I hadn't done anything wrong this time).

Then as soon as Mr Stilton started talking to the class Emily twisted her chair, turning her back on me.

It was just as well, though, because a moment later Notes popped out of her pen pot and plonked a note in front of me.

??? **Questionnaire** ???

① Is you is...
A. Miserables because of probabilities?
B. Miserables because is missing Chloe?
C. Miserables because is hungry?
D. Pretending miserables for acting practice?

② Is it you wants...
A. Helpings with maths?
B. Helpings with friendlings?
C. Double helpings of puddings?

③ If you is being an animal, which animal is you is?

A. A millipede with plenty legs for extra good countings?
B. A sad monkey with no monkey friendlings?
C. A bear which is not done eatings for looong times and is now having bad thinkings about yummy rabbits and fishies?
D. A famous zebra?

Madness. I turned the paper

over and wrote ...

You could just
ask what's up?

Also, I'm fine.
Nothing's up.

Not really true but

I didn't want to talk

about it.

She turned over the

paper and pointed.

"OK, OK ..." I whispered.

I looked at the questions again. Where was

the option for "None of these crazy answers has

anything to do with how I'm feeling"? But if I

had to pick ... if I absolutely had to ...

Well, I definitely wasn't worried about maths.
And I'm ALWAYS hungry so that was nothing
new. And, no, I didn't want to be

A famous Zebra

(or even a famous human).

1. B

2. B/C
(because I really
don't think you
can help, and I
really do like
puddings).

Notes nodded as
she read my answers, then
scrawled a message underneath.

3. B

Is as I thinked!
My clever questings is reveals
the secret truth → Molly needs
another friend(ing!
But is OK, Molly Mills!
Notes will do super-helpings!!

Uh-oh. As I said, Notes' helpings weren't
always helpful.

CHAPTER THREE

I wanted to tell Notes not to help. I shook my head and even picked up a bit of paper to write the words "PLEASE DON'T".

I got as far as this:

PLEASE
DO

But before I could add the extremely important "N'T" part, Notes jumped on her pencil and whizzed away! I jumped up to find her, scraping my chair and (totally accidentally) making Emily squeal. But I quickly sat down when I saw that Mr Stilton was talking to the class again.

Across the room, Marvin Palmer poked his finger into the air, bopping his head from side to side.

"Marvin, is your hand up?" said Mr Stilton.

Marvin looked surprised. "No!" he said. "Was doing the Fizz."

"The what?"

"It's a dance," said Marvin, still bopping. "I was doing it in my head, then my body joined in. *Rewind time!*"

He made a weird *zip-zup-zip* sound, put his arm down and sat on his hand.

"We need to move on," sighed Mr Stilton.

Mr Stilton never knows what to say to Marvin.

Marvin is what my nan would call "a right character", which basically means he's a bit different. I like him. Everyone likes him. But he's hard to talk to because he's mostly thinking about something totally different to what you're saying.

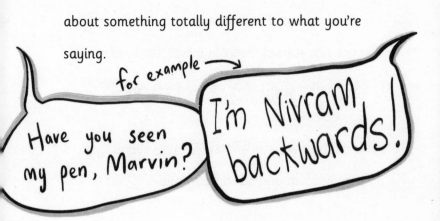

for example →

Have you seen my pen, Marvin?

I'm Nivram backwards!

"OK, back to maths. Yes, Emily?"

"There's a five out of six chance of not getting a six," said Emily.

But then instead of saying well done to Emily, Mr Stilton looked over at me and said, "Molly, I have to say, I'm pleasantly surprised at your teaching skills." Even though I had nothing to do with it.

And this got Emily so mad that the muscle in her jaw started clenching, and her nostrils started flaring, so I thought I should probably say something.

"I didn't do anything," I said.

But Mr Stilton said, "Now, now, don't be modest. In fact, here's an idea. There's a spare seat at your table ... Marvin, why don't you join Molly and Emily?"

"But what about Saffire?!" I said quite loudly.

Oops.

"Huh?" said everyone.
(Everyone except Marvin, who said, "Kapow!")

"Doesn't matter," I mumbled.

I shuffled my stuff to one side so Marvin could sit down and smiled at him. It wasn't his fault he wasn't a **cool new flashy-named friend.**

While this was going on, Notes was behaving VERY strangely. She was flying all over the room, darting from table to table on her magic pencil. Luckily I'm the only one who can see her (except for Chloe ... sigh!) or else everyone would have been proper freaking.

She was up to something for sure. Something well meaning but totally over the top knowing Notes. I had a horrible feeling she was about to make me look like a big weirdy weirdo.

I missed Chloe. I missed writing notes about the stuff that was bothering me.

Maybe I could try writing to Marvin?

Marvin,
do you ever feel like something embarrassing is going to happen and there's absolutely nothing you can do about it?

Marvin looked at me, confused. Then he laughed. **"Beans, beans, good for your heart. The more you eat the more you—"**

"Yeah, not *that* sort of embarrassing," I said. "More like someone's going to do something to embarrass you or ... I can't really explain it."

Marvin looked around suspiciously. He lifted his hands into a karate pose and started air-chopping, like he was fighting off my enemies for me. Which made me smile but wasn't particularly helpful.

Writing to Marvin wasn't going to work.

Anyway, maths was all the same kind of thing
— like, **what's the probability of
rolling two sixes?**

**What's the probability of rolling
three sixes?**

**What's the probability of me ever
making another best friend?**

(Actually, that wasn't one of the questions,
but I would still like to know the answer.)

While I was trying

to figure out all this dice stuff, Notes was still

busy swooping and swooshing around the room.

I thought about chasing after her, but then got distracted, because Adam W. from Mrs Banton's class knocked on the door and said something VERY interesting.

"Sir," he said, "Mrs Banton needs your list of names for the Inter-cool ... I mean, the Intra-cruel ... I mean, the spelling competition."

"Spelling competition?" said Mr Stilton. "I don't know anything about it."

"Mrs Banton said you, er, might say that," said Adam W. "She said to look in your pile."

Mr Stilton always has a pile on his desk. There can be letters, books, forms, posters, leaflets and all sorts in that pile, and it just grows bigger and bigger until we get to the weekend. Then by Monday it has shrunk again.

Anyway, he gritted his teeth and started rummaging in the pile. "I can assure you there's nothing here about a spelling competition," he said, right before he pulled out a massive poster.

"Oh, that," he mumbled. "Fine."

Then he boomed at the class, "Pens down, mouths closed, eyes on me! Hands up, who wants to compete in a spelling competition?"

INTER-SCHOOL
SPELLING
CHAMPIONSHIPS

10am May 12th
Bogdale Hall

Compete against the
BEST YOUNG SPELLERS
in Bogdale!

Win a sense of deep
pride and satisfaction!

Emily's hand zoomed up, followed by maybe half the class.

"A spelling competition in front of parents and teachers," he said.

A bunch of kids lowered their hands.

"A chance to compete against the best young spellers in Bogdale," he continued.

More kids lowered their hands.

"The top speller will win—"

The few kids who still had their hands up suddenly sat straighter, eyes wide, holding their breath.

Mr Stilton frowned at the poster.

"A sense of deep pride and satisfaction," he said (and I'm sure I heard him mumble something about tight-fisted cheapskates).

The remaining kids put their hands down in disgust.

All except for Emily, of course.

"You're sure?!" asked Mr Stilton, looking over at our table.

"Definitely!" said Emily.

"Not you, Emily. Of course you're doing it. I meant our other volunteer."

"I don't understand," she said, but then she saw it ... my hand ... me.

Because if Chloe could be all **cool** and **no-big-deal** about this spelling thing, so could I. If she was into doing new stuff with her new friends, well, so what, **me too!**

Except – one small problem – I didn't have any new friends, and I still hated spelling tests.

Also, I was struggling with the whole **cool** and **no-big-deal** thing.

My throat was all tight and my mouth was drier than a **cream cracker.**

"I-I'm sure," I said.

I really, REALLY wasn't.

CHAPTER FOUR

At lunchtime everyone hurried out, but I hung back to look for Notes.

I gave up after about two seconds, though, because I found this sticking out of the pen pot:

← Paper wasn't there before!

READ ME!

I is off doing wondrous helpings!
I is been seetings and searchings
for Molly's brand-new
splendid friendling!

Molly's friendling MUST has (some.)
same likes as Molly.

I has checked all childings
in Molly's class and has picked
five super-best ones!
Checkings is in Molly's notepad
if wants to see.

More helpings soon!
Byezeees!

Checkings? Checkings?! I

had a bad feeling about these checkings!

My notepad was sticking out of my fluffy dog

pencil case like it had recently been used. But

before I had a chance to look, Mr Stilton said,

"Out you go, Molly."

Which totally made me jump because I'd forgotten he was even in the room.

He'd already pulled a battered white lunch box from his desk drawer and was miserably prodding something gloopy with a fork.

Ick.

I quickly took my own lunch box from my locker, then I hurried out.

Everywhere was busy. I squeezed onto a picnic table and started stuffing food into my mouth. All I really wanted to do was look at my notepad, but we're not allowed to go off and play until we've eaten.

So I ate crazy fast.

 cheese sandwich
(gobble, gulp, gone in five bites),

 crisps (crunch, munch, down the hatch),

 banana (nom, nom, oops – ate a mushy bit),

 apple juice (suck, slurp, done!),

 wrinkly thing
(chomp, chew ... ew ... old raisin.
How did that get in there?!).

I slam-dunked my rubbish
into the big hippo-
shaped bin,
then
clicked
my lunch
box shut. It was only
when I got up to go that
I realised everyone at
the picnic table
was staring.

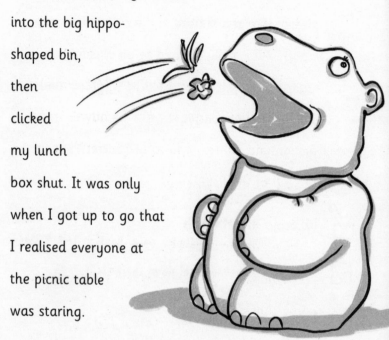

Oops. Bit embarrassing.

"I'm in a rush," I mumbled, like that wasn't totally obvious already.

Then I ran. I ran straight past Mrs Guthman, the dinner lady, straight past the adventure playground, all the way to the Secret Spot at the far end of the field.

Being at the Secret Spot without Chloe was pretty horrible, but there was no time to think about that.

My fingers were already turning the blue-lined pages of my notepad. My eyes were already scanning ... searching ... and then I saw them. Page after page. Checkings after checkings.

pencil toppings X
fluffy stuffs X
Crispies X
Other stuffs... ??
Huh?!
?!!
isha
4
3
her stuffs:
ingings
unnings
Harry
meany
grinnings: 4
Trustables: 0
Grumplings: 5
truthness: 1
5
5
5

Same likings

pencil toppings ✓
fluffy stuffs ✗
crispies ✓
Other stuffs ⟿ Making paper planes

DAISY
Grinnings: 4
trustables: 4
Truthness:
Grumps:

ALFIE
3

Grinnings →
trustable
Trusting
grump

MARVIN
Grinnings: 5
Trustables: 5
Truthness: 4
Grumplings = 0 !!!
Has same likes
↓ ↓ ↙
• pencil toppings ✓
• crispies ✓
• Chloe ?

5
♡

5 ♡

Emily
Grinnings: 2
Trustables: 5
truthness: 5
Grumplings:
Likes

Oh. Oh, wow. OK. I put a hand on my chest and felt as my heart slowed from a frantic bubbada-bubbada to a normal human boom-ba-boom, boom-ba-boom.

This was OK. Notes hadn't actually done anything. As far as I could tell, she'd just watched all (and I mean ALL!) the kids in my class and written a bunch of funny little lists.

I remembered what she'd said about picking the five super-best ones. Who were they? Marvin's checkings looked pretty great

(which makes sense because he *is* pretty great),

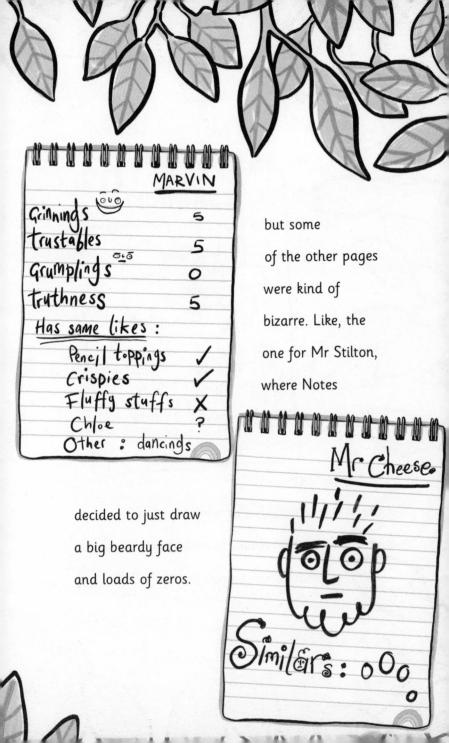

MARVIN

Grinnings	5
trustables	5
Grumplings	0
truthness	5

Has same likes:

Pencil toppings	✓
Crispies	✓
Fluffy stuffs	✗
Chloe	?
Other : dancings	

but some of the other pages were kind of bizarre. Like, the one for Mr Stilton, where Notes

decided to just draw a big beardy face and loads of zeros.

Mr Cheese.

Similars: o o o

Or the one for the spider

that lives in the book corner.

Madam Hairy Legs

Similars: ? ? ?
(Must asks does friendling
Molly likes munchy
flies!)

I wanted to read the whole lot in

one go. After all, I still didn't know

who Notes' top five were, did I? But

something was nagging at me. I still hadn't
written back to Chloe. She'd be expecting a reply
and I wanted to get it over and done with.

So even though I was not *at all* in a good,
happy, friendly-writing mood, I began …

Chloe,
Hey, big ~~coinsidents~~ ~~coincidence~~ funny thing
– I'm doing that spelling competition too.
I mean, I know I used to hate spelling tests,
but I've changed a lot since you were here.

Also, I have a new friend called Saffire. She
sits next to me now. She's hilarious. Everyone
wants to be her friend, but she really just likes
hanging out with me.

Love from Molly

I know what you're thinking. I lied. I lied to my (possibly ex) best friend. Yep, I know, I know. Bad thing to do.

There's no excuse really, but I was upset. She didn't need me any more and I wanted it to seem like I didn't need her either. I'm not proud of myself.

I folded the note carefully into a paper plane and jotted "Chloe" on the outside.

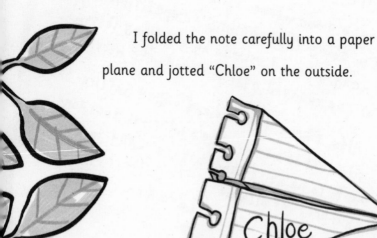

Then I picked up my things and climbed out of
the Secret Spot ...

... and this is what I saw:

What. Was. Happening?!?

Paper planes were darting everywhere. I
counted one ... two ... at least five of them! This

had to have something to do with Notes.

The field was busy with kids now, and loads were pointing up, staring.

Were these all for me? Maybe they were from Chloe ... but no, if they were for me, then why were they dancing all over the place?

Where was Notes?

Then I saw my little scribble witch friend, a tiny dot in the sky at first, getting nearer and nearer. And soon she was close enough that I could see her properly, flying on her pencil, a huge grin on her little face. She flew straight

over, and all the while the paper planes kept on ducking and diving. They loop-the-looped above the kids' heads like playful little birds.

"What's going on?!" I said as Notes settled on my shoulder.

She winked at me, then she pointed at the paper planes. Her finger began to shimmer and shine. And

ZIPPERTY-ZAP!

tiny golden lights darted towards them.

I yelped!

(It was freaky, OK?! I mean, my friend suddenly had an electric finger! Or possibly not electric but *definitely* magic and RIGHT NEXT TO MY FACE!)

One by one the paper planes stopped mid-air.
Then they turned, each pointing in a different
direction.

And

Down they went!

One landed in Alfie's pocket. Another landed
in Grace's big hair bow. Another – I THINK –
prodded Marvin in the bottom (I saw him rubbing
it, so that's what I'm guessing happened). I didn't
see where the others went, but I had a good
idea.

"Notes?" I said. "Those paper planes were

letters, weren't they? You sent them to five kids in my class, didn't you ... the five who scored best in the checkings?"

Notes skipped down on to my hand and tugged at my notepad. I gave it to her and immediately she flipped it open.

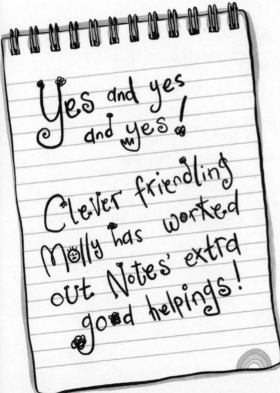

Yes and yes and yes!

Clever friendling Molly has worked out Notes' extra good helpings!

"Oh, Notes! What did you write?!"

She smiled, yawned, flipped the pad to a new page.

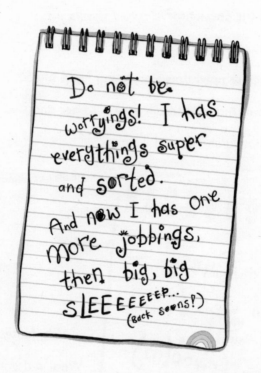

Do not be. worryings! I has everythings super and sorted. And now I has one more jobbings, then big, big SLEEEEEEEP... (Back soons?)

"What? No ... no more jobbings! Oh, that ..."

I realised Notes had seen my paper plane. The one for Chloe. I wasn't sure I even wanted to send it any more. *Maybe I should just write another one*, I thought. I should just tell her I missed her and that I was lonely, because that was the truth, wasn't it?

But Notes had already grabbed her pencil and clambered on to the Chloe-plane.

"Oh!" I said. "Wait!"

She paused, and I almost told her not to go. Almost.

But then I thought about Chloe's flashy new

friends and the sensible bit of my brain stopped working.

Notes raised a doodly eyebrow at me, clearly wondering what I was thinking.

"I just wanted to say ... safe flying," I said.

She grinned. Then off she flew, and it was too late to change my mind.

CHAPTER FIVE

I stayed at the Secret Spot until the bell went.
Partly I was thinking Chloe might write back (she
didn't). Partly I just wanted to hide. I didn't know
what Notes had written on those paper planes,
but it was definitely about me.

And I was right to be worried. Because the
moment I stepped inside the classroom
everything got weird.

Marvin was already at our table, busy fiddling
with a piece of paper.

He grinned when he saw me. "Friendling!" he said.

Uh-oh, I thought. What did Notes write?!

Marvin held out the paper – the note – so I could see it.

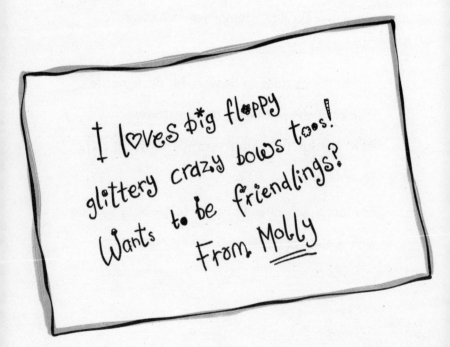

I loves big floppy glittery crazy bows toos! Wants to be friendlings? From Molly

Huh? Last time I checked Marvin was bow-free, un-bowed, bowless. This note clearly wasn't meant for him. The only person I knew with a big glittery bow was Grace.

I looked over to Grace's table. There she was, hunched over a piece of paper, a huge bow clipped in her hair. But if Marvin had Grace's note, what was she reading?

Along with the bow, Grace also wore a VERY confused frown. I watched as she wrote something underneath the note.

Then she folded it back into a paper plane.

She looked up, checked Mr Stilton wasn't

looking, then threw it at me.

Helloo∞!
Computings is wœndrous,
isn't they? And your
robot doodlings is sooo∞o
good!
I do doodles toos but
not robots.
Wants be friendlings?
        Mally

Was this meant for Alfie?
He's the robot doodler.
    You OK? I'm so confused!!
        Grace
          x

"Sorry!" I mouthed.

She shrugged. She looked like she was trying not to laugh.

Urgh.

Had to focus. Grace had Alfie's note, so next stop, Alfie.

Mr Stilton was busy dealing with some lunchtime drama. I could see him **waggling his finger** at Maryam and Aisha. So I took the opportunity to nip out of my seat and visit Alfie's table.

Alfie was scratching his head and – of course – reading a note.

"Hi," I said, "w-what's that you've got?"

He looked up with a befuddled smile and held out the note. "I think this is meant for someone else," he said.

How many times was I going to have to do this?

I thought. It was all SO embarrassing!

"Yeah," I said. "Sorry," I said. "Thanks," I said.

Turning away, I scanned the note.

Hizees!
I hates the spellings too!
Wants be friendlings?
Molly

Argh.

"All right, you horrible grottlings!" said Mr Stilton. (OK, fine, he didn't say that out loud, but he may as well have.) "Sit down, settle down and quieten down for register."

I slunk back towards my table. Halfway there, I heard a "Pssst". Mia, who sits on the next table, handed me ANOTHER note. Oh, crumbs.

I quickly read ...

Helloo*!
*You is doing the fizz so wells!
And you is super grinny!
Be friendlings?
Molly

On the back was:

Helo,
Is this ment
for Marvin?
You alrite?
Mia
x

Ah, well at least
now I knew
someone else who
didn't like spelling.

"Yeah, thanks," I mumbled. I tried to smile but I must've looked really odd.

By now my cheeks were so hot you could've cooked pancakes on them. Plus, my jaw was tense from all the cringing.

So I probably looked a lot like this:

Which explains why Mia then looked like this:

Scared smile

Urgh. Urgh. Urgh.

I shuffled back to my seat and stuffed the notes into my pencil case.

At least I had all of them now. Mia had Marvin's note, so it had gone full circle.

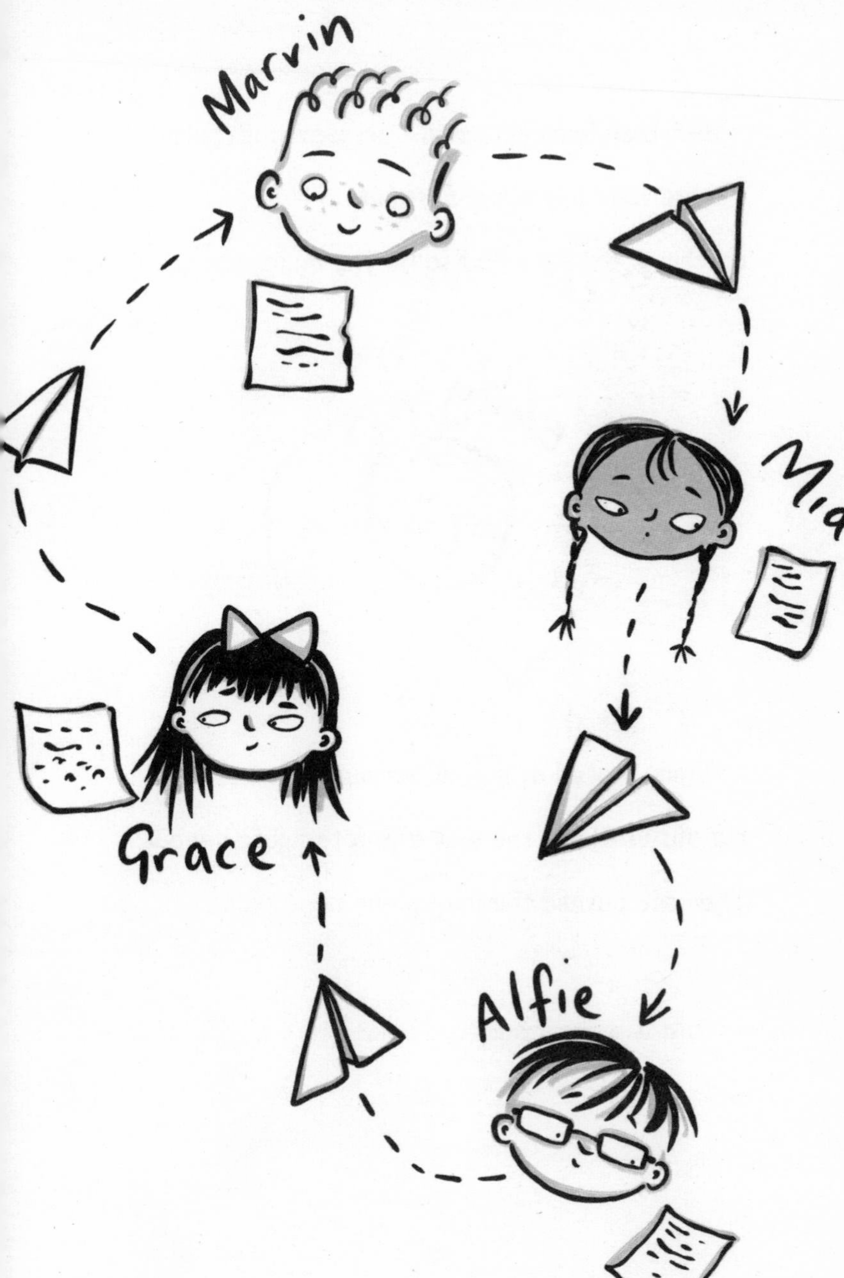

Marvin
Mia
Grace
Alfie

But then I remembered — oh, yeah, of course
— there were five *super-best kids* in Notes'
checkings, so there had to be one more note ...

Emily looked at me, all serious. It was a long,
curious look, like she was trying to figure me out.
Then she pushed the final plane towards me.

This is what it said ...

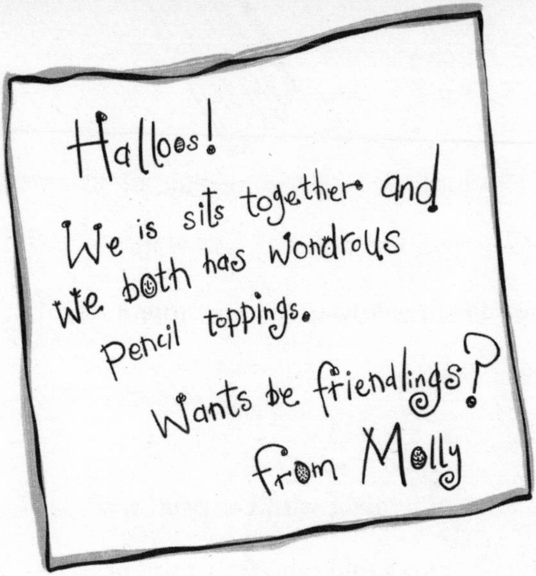

Halloos!
We is sits together and
we both has wondrous
pencil toppings.

Wants be friendlings?
From Molly

I turned it over and read her reply.

Is this about earlier?
We're still friends,
OK? I was just having
a bad morning.
                    E x

I pulled a scrap from the

corner of the paper.

Cool.
M x

Oh well — at least that was sorted.

Me and Emily will never be best friends but I still kind of like her.

Emily started fiddling with her pens and pencils again, and I told myself to calm down about the whole note thing.

It was no big deal, was it? Just a few notes sent to the wrong people. By paper plane. With no explanation. Written in Notes' funny-talk writing.

Urgh. This so *was* a big deal.

My cheeks were all hot and I had that horrible, **jittery** feeling you get when too many people are looking at you.

Then, just as I was totally failing to chill out, a sudden swoosh of air by my right ear made me flinch. It was Notes!

Something in me relaxed a bit.

My little paper witch friend was back! Though this time there was no paper plane ...

No letter from Chloe.

Oh.

This probably had nothing to do with me mentioning my new (and imaginary) bestie, I told myself. Probably Chloe was just busy. Probably.

Anyway, there wasn't time to regret lying about new friends with fancy names. Because Notes had immediately noticed her crumpled notes sticking out of my pencil case.

She looked at me with big concerned eyes.

"There was a bit of a mix-up ..."

Mr Stilton began calling the register.

Whispering, I told Notes what had happened.

Her tiny jaw dropped as I explained that she'd sent the notes to the wrong kids.

Then, grabbing her magic pencil, all frantic and horrified, she wrote across the table.

I is sooo sorrying for muddles!! Notes just wanted to helps. But Notes has mades Molly feels even badser.

"Don't worry," I whispered. "It's not that bad."

It was that bad. Half the class now thought I was a **GIANT WEIRDO.** But there was no point making Notes feel even more guilty.

Anyway, that afternoon was going to be really busy. We had book reviews to write and a science investigation to start. So maybe if everyone had stuff to do ... maybe if I stayed really quiet ... maybe if I didn't draw any attention to myself ... maybe all the notesy weirdness would be forgotten. Maybe.

CHAPTER SIX

After register, Alfie and Maryam handed out the book-review sheets.

"Pick your favourite book and tell us what's so great about it," said Mr Stilton.

Great, I thought. *Easy*, I thought.

"But not you two." Mr Stilton waved a couple of huge books at me and Emily.

"You've got revision to do," he said.

"Huh?" I replied.

"Here," he said. He plonked the books in front of us.

Emily clapped her hands in excitement. "Ooh, an encyclopedia!" she gushed.

"A what?!? What's an **en-cycle-pee-dear?!**"

Mr Stilton sighed. "Encyclopedia, Molly. You should probably learn to spell it. These are books full of information, full of definitions, full of wonder," he said. "They're what people used before the internet."

"Oh," I said.

Did he want me to write a book review for this thing? That could be tricky.

Emily already had her nose in her encyclopedia and was eagerly turning the pages.

"But what do I *do* with it?" I said.

Mr Stilton slowed down his speech like he was talking to a really stupid person.

"You read it, Molly. You practise your spellings."

"Oh. Wouldn't a dictionary be better?" I said.

He glared at me, and I remembered **(too late)** that I had accidentally broken the last dictionary in our class. Though, just to be clear, I am totally not sorry about breaking it because:

1. It wasn't really my fault. Old things break.

2. When it broke, a bit of paper fell out. But it wasn't a page of dictionary, it was a drawing of a scribbly little witch (guess who?!). And when I cut the witch out **MAGIC HAPPENED!!!** And that's how Notes came to life.

(So, like I said, totally not sorry!)

"This'll be fine," I said.

"Excellent," he said. "We'll have a trial run in half an hour. Our own little classroom spelling contest. Give you two a chance to practise, eh?"

"Yes!!!" went Emily.

"Meh!" went me.

Oh, perfect. A spelling test in front of the whole class. Just what I needed.

Now I'd look like a weirdo *and* a loser.

My best day ever. NOT!

The encyclopedia was actually pretty cool.
Way better than a dictionary because there
were pictures. I would have enjoyed reading it.
Would have. But obviously I had the whole

SPELLING TEST OF **DOOM**

to prepare for, so that kind of ruined the fun.

Anyway, I learnt some new words. Go, me.

Turn over for my NEW WORD top ten!

10. Aardvark
(because of the cuteness)

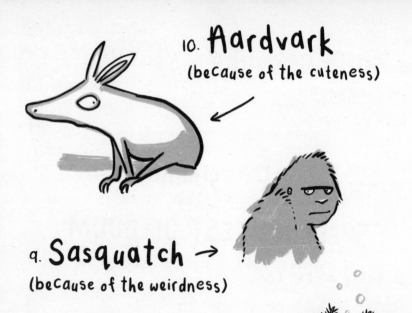

9. Sasquatch →
(because of the weirdness)

8. Axolotyl
(Best. Animal. Ever.)

7. Bacterium
(one little tiny bit of an illness.
All alone. Aw!)

6. Knickerbockers →
(big baggy trousers)

5. Knickerbocker glory
(big ice cream ... not to be confused with number 6!)

 ← 4. **Persimmon**
(fancy fruit)

3. Balaclava →

(like a sock but for keeping your head warm)

2. Theremin
(musical instrument made of magic)

1st **Encyclopedia**
(no explanation necessary)

Top Spot

Good, huh?! Not that I'd remember any of those spellings. And even if I did, so what? This seemed like the most pointless thing ever. There are literally **squillions** of words. It's not like I could learn all of them. I could spend hours and hours practising and still not know the ones in the competition, so what was the point in trying at all?!

"How's it going?" I asked Emily.

"Shh!" she said, not even looking up.

She looked like she was halfway through the book already. Had she learnt all those words? How?!

Maybe I was doing it wrong. What if I stared really hard and flicked the pages really fast? Maybe the words would zoom into my brain.

No. That didn't seem to work.

What if I rested my head on it like a pillow? Maybe the spellings would seep through my skull. That could work.

Hmm.

For a book it was surprisingly comfy. A big wordy book-pillow.

All that worrying was exhausting.

Through sleepy eyes I watched as Notes picked up her magic pencil.

She scrawled across the table:

Sleeps is wondrous for learnings...

Then she drew this:

"Silly Notes," I muttered. "I'm ... not sleeping ... just ... resting my eyeballs ..."

But obviously I did fall asleep. Because the next thing I remember is Notes prodding me and Mr Stilton yelling.

"If Molly and Emily would like to come to the front ..." said Mr Stilton.

Notes hopped on to my shoulder, holding her magic pencil. Then, on wobbly legs, I followed Emily.

My eyes were still a bit **BLURRY** and I could feel a massive yawn bubbling inside me.

"Do try to stay awake for this," Mr Stilton said when I reached the front of the class.

"I wasn't sleeping," I said.

But the yawn was still there, and it wanted to come out.

No, I thought. *I won't let it,* I thought.

Big mistake.

The problem is, if you tell a yawn it's got to stay inside you, it turns into the **hugest most jaw-gaping yawn** you've ever had.

I managed to hold it in while Mr Stilton told everyone to ...

"**Listen up!** Molly and Emily are about to go head to head in the most exciting spelling test of their lives!"

But then this happened.

Everyone laughed. Everyone except Mr Stilton.

"Molly," he said, "this may be your only
opportunity to practise before the real thing. The

Inter-School Spelling Championship is tomorrow!
Please focus!"

"Sorry," I mumbled.

He passed each of us a whiteboard and pen.

"I'm not sure exactly how it'll happen
tomorrow," said Mr Stilton, "but, for now, just
jot your answers on these and show them when I
say so. OK?"

"Perfect," smiled Emily.

I didn't say anything.

"OK, first word ..." said Mr Stilton.
"'Armadillo'."

Hmph, I thought. *So close to aardvark! Oh well.*

I did my best. You can kind of sound that one out.

"And show!" said Mr Stilton.

"Well done!" he said. "Next word ...

'Thoroughly'."

This one wasn't so easy. Notes climbed on to the whiteboard and tried to spell it, but hers was no better than mine.

"Too bad, Molly. Excellent work, Emily. Next word ..."

And that's how it went. Word after word after word.

This is how our boards looked.

I reminded myself this wasn't about winning.

This was about showing Chloe that I'd changed

... pretending that I didn't need her any more.

Mr Stilton didn't comment on my terrible score. And no one laughed, which I appreciated. In fact, when I got back to my seat, Marvin even gave me a high five. Maybe he didn't notice how badly I'd done.

Emily was all secret-smiles for the rest of the afternoon. Then, at the end of the day, she asked Mr Stilton if she could borrow an encyclopedia for the evening.

That was what I was up against – that level of keen.

I was going to look like such an **IDIOT.**

Right before we left, Mr Stilton announced
that he'd be driving the minibus tomorrow.

"As so few Dungfields pupils are in the
competition, there are spaces for anyone who'd
like to come and watch," he said, waving a
handful of permission letters. "Take one of these
if you'd like to come. The rest of you will be
doing art with Miss Rose."

Art (my favourite subject) with Miss Rose
(my favourite teacher) ... **THiS SO WASN'T FAiR!**

"Emily and Molly, you'll need a different
letter. Here."

"Why?" I said. "Oh ..."

Oh no. **NO, NO, NO.** As I looked at the

letter one sentence jumped out at me.

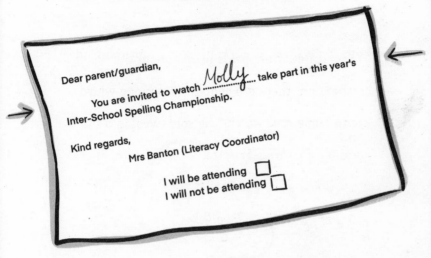

Dear parent/guardian,

You are invited to watch *Molly* take part in this year's
Inter-School Spelling Championship.

Kind regards,

Mrs Banton (Literacy Coordinator)

I will be attending ☐
I will not be attending ☐

With all the other stuff happening, I'd

forgotten Mum and Dad would be invited to see

me F-A-I-L ...

CHAPTER SEVEN

I didn't sleep too well that night. I kept thinking

of more and more words I couldn't spell.

terrable ✗
horrable ✗

And I kept thinking about that silly letter I

wrote to Chloe.

Chloe

One thing had worked out OK, though. Mum and Dad had promised NOT to go to the spelling competition. That would have been *too* awful.

I had very calmly asked them to tick the *will not be attending* box ...

"You can't come! Please don't come!! I'm going to be terrible!!! If you love me even a tiny bit, you'll STAAAY AWAAAAY!!!!"

... and they agreed. **PHEW.**

I said all this to Emily just before the morning bell went.

"Sorry to hear they're not coming," she said.

She looked really miserable about it, which was weird. It was like she hadn't really been listening.

"Huh?" I said. "I'm not sorry!"

"Oh," she said in a sad, faraway voice. Then she walked off.

And I thought I was strange! Who knew what that was about?

Anyway, a really weird thing happened when I got to class. Notes was there of course, sitting on the edge of the pen pot, stroking Captain Purrkins. She'd made all this good-luck bunting and decorated the class with it, which had Mr Stilton totally confused because no one was supposed to be in class last night. But that wasn't even the **weird** thing.

The **weird** thing was that there were kids giving in permission slips.

I should explain. When Mr Stilton asked if anyone wanted to watch the spelling competition, I just assumed no one would come. Why *would* they come? Pretty boring, isn't it, watching people trying to spell stuff?

Well, apparently Marvin didn't think it was boring. Mia didn't either. Or Alfie. Or Grace. Because they were all coming to watch the spelling competition.

Odd, I thought. Especially after the notes chaos.

Maybe they were friends with Emily. Not that I ever really saw her hanging around with anyone ... but maybe I just hadn't noticed.

Once I'd **stuffed** my coat in my locker, I went to see Notes. Dumping my pencil case on the table, I pulled out my notepad and flicked to a clean page.

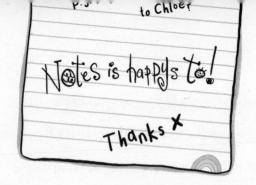

It was a short message, so it didn't take long

to write:

I should have just admitted how I was feeling (jealous, lonely ... all that fun stuff) and I very almost did. But then I started thinking of the what ifs ...

What if she thought I was babyish? ← Which I'm not ... I'm the opposite of babyish ... if anything, I'm oldish.

What if she laughed at me with her (probably horrible) new friends??

What if Chloe really *didn't* want to be friends any more???

So that's why I just sent a rubbish little nothing-note (not to be confused with the very unrubbish Notes with a big N).

Notes watched me writing the nothing-note.
She watched and she frowned. It was a seriously
unimpressed frown.

Molly is forgettings to be
wondrolls friendling
for Chloe!

She wrote that across the table, then stood
there waiting, hands on hips.

I was too sad to explain, so I
just shrugged and looked away.

But she took it anyway. She folded it into a tiny plane, grabbed her pencil and her cat and hopped aboard.

My scribble witch friend gave a final sad shake of the head, then she **ZOOMED** out of an open window.

I hardly spoke to anyone that morning. Emily was busy silently practising her spellings. She was doing this closed-eyes moving-lips thing, so I guessed she wouldn't want to chat. And Marvin was out of class doing whatever Marvin does out of class. (He goes out for a bit most days.)

So I just sat in silence through Maths, while

Mr Stilton talked about tessellating shapes. He showed us a clever drawing where this bird shape was repeated over and over.

He told us to copy it, which normally would be my dream Maths lesson. I **LOVE** drawing anything. But it wasn't going too well.

Some bits fitted together really well, but other bits wouldn't. The problem was that all my birds were slightly different. So one bird's wing fitted with another bird's tummy perfectly, but then that bird's tail wouldn't fit with the next bird's beak.

And I was too busy worrying about all the

Chloe-Saffire-Daffodil-spelling-competition

awfulness to really give the drawing my full

attention.

I wondered if Chloe would write back to me.
I didn't think she would. I hoped it but didn't
believe it.

She did write, though. Eventually. But I'll get
to that ...

It was a little while later. Marvin was back in
class and Mr Stilton had just told all the spelling-
competition kids to get their coats on.

"We're leaving in five minutes, so if you need the toilet, make it **quick!**" he'd said.

As I didn't need the loo I dawdled at the lockers. I pulled on my jacket and stared at the open window, wishing Notes would come back.

Where was she?

I needed her at the competition with me. Who else would hug my nose when I lost? Who else would write me little notes saying it would all be OK?

Another thought occurred. What if she abandoned me for Chloe? She was Chloe's friend too, after all. I shouldn't have felt jealous at the idea, but I did.

Adam W. and a couple of others from Mrs Banton's class lurked by the door, ready to go.

"Right!" said Mr Stilton. He did a quick head count, then announced, **"WE'RE OFF!"**

Miss Rose had already taken over teaching our class. The Art lesson looked so much fun. Junk-modelling. We NEVER got to do junk-modelling any more. For the GAZILLIONTH time I wished I could stay.

But Mr Stilton was already marching out of the door, the rest of the group trailing after him. I gave the open window a final miserable glance, then I followed.

Notes wasn't coming.

CHAPTER EIGHT

It wasn't until I was aboard the minibus that I saw her. I sat at the back of the bus, staring out of the rear window. And at first, when I saw a little speck in the sky, I thought I was just imagining it, because I wanted her there so much.

But she got closer and closer, and it was definitely her! And she was definitely riding a paper plane. **A MESSAGE FROM CHLOE!**

But she was too late. The minibus doors were shut. The windows had been jammed for years. There was no way in!

It felt horrible leaving without her.

I breathed on the rear-window glass and wrote with my finger...

Though, as the minibus pulled away, something happened ... Notes' eyes became fiercely focused ... she leaned forward on the plane ... and ...

WHOOOOOSH!

In a rush of speed she zoomed towards the minibus. She was coming after all! Flying along behind us!

But my excitement didn't last long. Notes was concentrating so hard on following the minibus that she didn't see the flock of pigeons about to

cut across her path.

Then **THWACK!** In a moment of papery-feathery terror Notes smacked into the side of a poor dozy bird.

Both went spiralling down.

"No!" I gasped. Twisting in my seat belt, I pressed my nose to the back window and could just about see Notes and the pigeon doddering at the roadside.

The dazed pair were soon tiny specks in the distance as the minibus hurried towards its destination.

I felt sick. I've never been great with journeys, but this wasn't travel sickness. This was "what if my friend is hurt?" sickness, which is

SO MUCH WORSE!!!

And then we stopped. The traffic lights had changed, and we sat there, engine humming, while I stared out at the road behind, searching for Notes.

Was she going to be OK? Would she find her way back to me? What was that scrunched-up paper thing flying through the air?

Wait ... **HUH?!**

It was Notes! There she was again! Notes herself was fairly crisp, but the paper plane now had a very crumpled-looking nose. Still, it was flying, and Notes was in one piece, so everything was OK.

Until it started raining.

Rain and paper witches DO NOT go together. So when tiny droplets began splattering the windows, I **100%** panicked.

"STOP THE BUS" I yelled.

"Someone pass Molly a sick bag!" yelled Mr Stilton, not even slowing.

"I don't need a sick bag; I need to get off!" I said. "Please!"

"We're almost there!" he shouted. "You're just nervous. Everyone keep your belts on!"

"It's OK, Molly. It's just spelling," said Alfie.

"But!?!" I said.

It was still raining, and I now couldn't see Notes.

"Anyway, we're here to cheer you on," said Mia.

"Yup, great ..." I said, still looking over my shoulder.

"We had a chat after the note thing yesterday," said Grace. "We didn't want you to be lonely or anything now that Chloe's gone."

"Got it. Not lonely," I said, but I wasn't really listening.

Not until Marvin leaned round his seat and yelled **"KAPOW!"** That got my attention.

And suddenly I got what they were saying. They'd come along to be my friends, and I was being totally ungrateful. After all, *they* didn't know I was stressing about Notes.

I forced my eyes away from the back window.

"Thank you," I said. "All of you. You're right ... I'm just a bit, er, worried ... about the competition ... and a bit lonely ... but it's better with you all here."

I hoped that sounded genuine, because I really did appreciate them coming, even though I was still **TOTALLY FREAKING OUT** about my scribble witch friend.

As Mr Stilton parked the minibus I wriggled in my seat, fingers twitching over my seat-belt button.

Then the moment he said, "OK, let's go," I was unclicked and out of that bus.

My heart **BOOM-BADOOMED** as I ran

out into the rain.

Notes was there in the air, though flying VERY

strangely.

"Wow, look!" said Alfie, as the paper plane

landed at our feet. "Who threw that?"

The plane was just normal paper, so of course people could see it. What they couldn't see was my tiny scribble witch friend or her pencil-topper cat.

I scooped up Notes and Captain Purrkins. I didn't care if I looked weird to the other kids, scooping up thin air.

I looked at them closely, sheltering them under my jacket. Notes still clutched her magic pencil but was shaking.

Poor little Notes! At least she wasn't soggy, though.

"You're dry?" I whispered.

She nodded.

"Are you OK, though? I saw you hit that
pigeon ... and then the funny way you were
flying ..."

She looked around for something to write on,
so I pulled up my sleeve. She could write on my
arm. I knew it wouldn't hurt, so long as she used
her magic pencil.

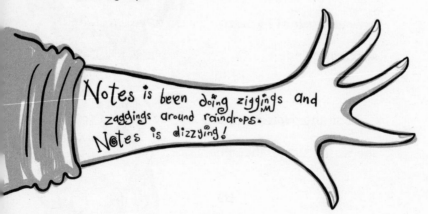

With that she swayed, then plonked down on to her bottom. Captain Purrkins didn't look too well either. He started gagging the way my nan's cat does when he's got a hairball. And then – **yuck!** – he gagged again and out it came. Though oddly this hairball looked a lot like the end of a pencil rubber. Anyway, he immediately plopped down on to Notes' lap and I gently put them both in my pocket.

It was only then that I realised there was a bit of a fuss going on over the paper plane.

In all the panic I'd forgotten Chloe's message.

Alfie saw me looking over. "I only opened it to see how it was made, but look!" he said.

He held out the note so I could read it. There wasn't much to read.

Yeah. You too.

The others stood around looking at the crumpled paper in frowny confusion ...

"Can I see?" I said.

With a shrug Alfie gave me the note, then turned his attention to Mr Stilton, who was calling us over.

I couldn't believe it. Was that really all Chloe had written? I turned it over, held it upside down, held it up to the (fairly dismal) light, shook it. But nope. Three words. Three rubbishy words.

Even I'd managed seven words. Three was just plain rude.

GRUMPING and **FUMING**, I joined the line of Dungfields kids. I'd been right all along. Chloe didn't care any more.

Well, then I'd show her just how much I didn't care either. I was a brand-new Molly with brand-new interests. And as Mr Stilton led us to the big open doors of Bogdale Hall I made myself a promise:

I WAS GOING TO WIN THIS COMPETITION.

winning attitude

(not sure where the headband came from)

CHAPTER NINE

SPOILER ALERT: I didn't win. What was I even thinking?!

Turns out promising yourself you're going to win something doesn't actually make it happen. Not without practice and talent and stuff.

(To be fair, our Dungfields motto, 'DREAM, DARE, DO', in no way mentions anything about actual work. So it's not entirely my fault the competition was a COMPLETE DISASTER.)

Here's what happened.

145

Emily and I ditched our coats and went up on to the stage with the other contestants, INCLUDING Chloe, who I had decided to ignore. This wasn't very nice of me, I know. I'm just telling it how it was.

I took Notes and Captain Purrkins with me, of course. Notes looked a bit less shaken now. She sat on my shoulder and waved at Chloe. I pretended not to notice.

A lady with a clipboard read our names out in alphabetical order and we had to line up with a whiteboard and pen.

She called "Molly Mills" and I went and stood

next to a boy called Zachary Macclesfield. Then she read out the next name. "Daffodil Nettles".

URGH, I thought. Chloe's new favourite person. Wonderful Daffodil. Great. (Again: not nice. I know, I know.)

"You're Chloe's friend," she said to me as she joined the line. She smiled.

I looked away.

Am I? I mumbled.

"What was that?" said Daffodil.

I didn't respond.

"I'm Daffodil," said Daffodil, clearly deciding to try again. "Chloe's told me so much about you. All the funny things you two got up to."

Daffodil was still smiling at me, even though I wasn't looking at her. I could see the glint of her white teeth in the corner of my vision.

And then the glint disappeared, and I heard her mumble, "Rude."

After that she stood as far away from me as

possible while still being next to me in the line.

I glanced at Chloe and saw her shrug at Daffodil and mouth the word "weird".

Then I noticed Notes had climbed on to my whiteboard and she had her unimpressed frown on again.

She shook her head as she wrote ...

Molly is forgottens niceness and kindings AGAIN!

I haven't. I'm just sad about Chloe not being my friend.

No, no, no! Sads is → Molly is jealousings!!

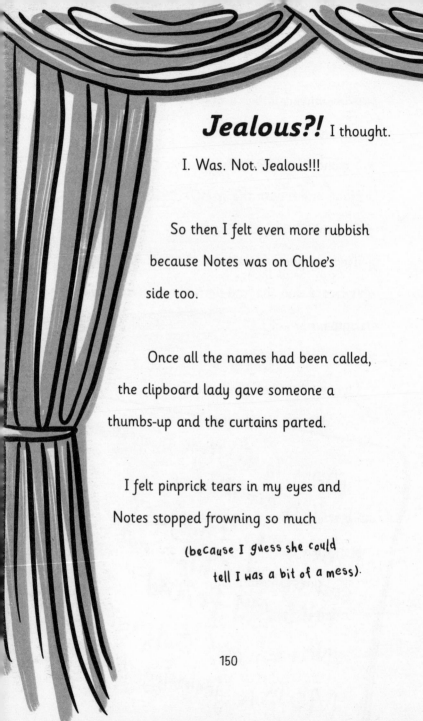

Jealous?! I thought.

I. Was. Not. Jealous!!!

So then I felt even more rubbish because Notes was on Chloe's side too.

Once all the names had been called, the clipboard lady gave someone a thumbs-up and the curtains parted.

I felt pinprick tears in my eyes and Notes stopped frowning so much (because I guess she could tell I was a bit of a mess).

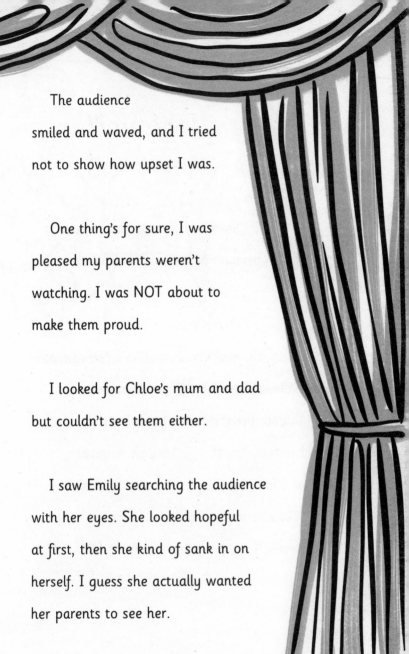

The audience
smiled and waved, and I tried
not to show how upset I was.

One thing's for sure, I was
pleased my parents weren't
watching. I was NOT about to
make them proud.

I looked for Chloe's mum and dad
but couldn't see them either.

I saw Emily searching the audience
with her eyes. She looked hopeful
at first, then she kind of sank in on
herself. I guess she actually wanted
her parents to see her.

"Welcome, everyone, to the fifth annual Inter-School Spelling Championship. As ever, we're delighted to be joined by the very best, keenest spellers in Bogdale," said the clipboard lady.

Uh-oh, I thought. The words "best" and "keenest" were definitely not me.

Notes looked at me and flexed
her muscles like she was telling me
to be strong.

**"The rules are as follows:
contestants are allowed one wrong
spelling. After that they will be asked to sit
down. The first round is a whiteboard round.
Children, please write your answers without
showing the contestants either side of you,
then when I say 'go', hold up your boards!"**

Daffodil wrote something on her board.

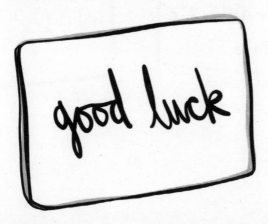

good luck

I ignored it.

"Round one," said the clipboard lady. **"The first word is 'INTERGALACTIC.'"**

I started writing. My first attempt looked a bit iffy, so I tried again.

Chloe loves space stuff, so straight away I knew she'd get it right. But when the clipboard lady said **"go"** I realised I was wrong.

Poor Chloe. It must have been extra horrible getting a space word wrong. It'd be like me getting a stationery word wrong (though, actually, 'stationery' is a really tricky word to spell).

I was still feeling huffy with Chloe, but now I also felt a tiny bit bad for her. I tried to give her a sympathetic smile, but she wasn't looking.

The clipboard lady put some ticks on her clipboard. **"Next,"** she said,

"spell 'EXTINCT.'"

Oh, yikes. I knew what it meant: gone for ever. But I couldn't spell it.

As it turns out, neither could Chloe.

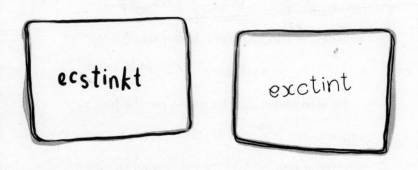

This time I felt *really* bad for Chloe, out in the first round. Again, I tried to catch her eye, but she wasn't looking.

And when she eventually did look over she looked at Daffodil, not me.

So then I looked at Daffodil and the look I gave her probably **(definitely)** wasn't very nice.

not my best moment ever

So then Notes started giving me the frowns again.

Chloe and another girl went to sit on the losers' bench, and the round continued.

"Spell 'DISAPPOINTED.'"

I was tempted to get it wrong on purpose so I could sit with Chloe. I didn't care about looking silly any more. But I figured I'd be on the bench soon enough anyway, so I might as well try.

I got it right. So did everyone else.

Someone in the audience shouted **"KAPOW!"**
And even though I still felt as nervous as my
gran's quivering guinea pig, I guess I also started
to feel a tiny bit Vikingish. Like ... like I was still
Ginny (that's the guinea pig's name by the way), but
now I was Ginny with cool horns. Anyway, it
helped a bit (thanks, Marvin!) until this:

"Round two!" said the clipboard lady.
**"Whiteboards down. In this round I'll ask you
to spell a word OUT LOUD, one contestant at
a time."**

My awesome,
imaginary horns poofed
into thin air! This was the
scary bit I'd been dreading. This was
the bit that made my throat tighten so much I
might not be able to get any letters out anyway!

I had ages before my turn came round. Each
time the clipboard lady asked someone to spell a
word, I'd try to spell it in my head. Not once did
I get it right. So when she eventually asked me
to spell "unsuccessful", I knew I was doomed.

'U-N-S-U-C-S-E-F-U-L-L?'

"Please sit down, Molly."

Fine, I thought. At least now I could sit near Chloe and maybe work out if she even slightly wanted to still be friends. But by now there were quite a few kids on the bench. Sulky kids. Sulky kids who wouldn't budge up so I could sit near my used-to-be-best friend. So I plonked myself down next to Adam W. from Mrs Banton's class (also sulking).

Notes followed me to the bench and perched on my knee, giving it a quick "never mind" squeeze.

Anyway, next it was Daffodil's turn.

"Daffodil, spell 'HORRENDOUS'," said the
clipboard lady.

Daffodil closed her eyes like she was trying to
focus.

Her lips moved like she was trying to
remember the letters, but no sound came out.
Eventually she said, "Horrendous:

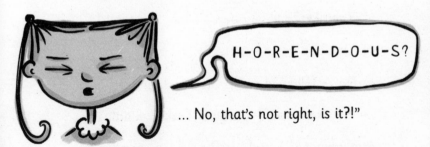

H-O-R-E-N-D-O-U-S?

... No, that's not right, is it?!"

Clipboard lady shook her head. **"No, I'm
sorry, Daffodil,"** she said, and Daffodil slumped

over towards the losers' bench. She sat down next to me and looked at me, though I kept on staring forward, pretending she didn't exist. But I could feel her eyes burning into the side of my head, and eventually I *had* to look at her because it was getting weird.

"What?!" I whispered.

Then Daffodil whispered back, "Horrendous: M-O-L-L-Y-M-I-L-L-S."

Notes gasped. My cheeks flushed. I didn't know what to say. I was **hot**. I was **shaking**. I *was* horrendous. **I had to get away!!!**

My blood was pumping far too fast. My eyes
flitted about the hall, looking for an escape.

"I need the loo!" I yelled to the

clipboard lady.

Then I got up from the bench and ran!
Off the stage, past the gawping audience,
towards the toilets.

Though as I pushed
through the toilet
door I could've sworn
I heard a familiar voice
coming from the hall.

"Me too!" it said.

CHAPTER TEN

"Are you OK?" said Chloe, because the voice (of course) had been hers.

I shook my head, spraying the room with tears.

"What's going on, Molly? Why were you mean to Daffodil? Why were you mean to me?!"

"I didn't mean to be mean. I mean ... not to you. Maybe to Daffodil," I said. "I'm sorry. It's just you ... you ... you've changed! You're volunteering for spelling competitions and—"

"But you volunteered too!" she pointed out.

"Only because you did! I hate spelling. *You* used to hate spelling. But now you've got all these new, amazing friends, and you're different!"

"I'm not different! I still hate spelling. And anyway, you've got a new friend too. What about her?!"

"Oh ..." I said. I'd forgotten about Saffire.

Over Chloe's shoulder I could see Notes, writing on a cubicle door.

tells the truthful

Urgh, fine, I thought …

"Truth is," I said. I took a deep, *deeeeeeeep* breath. "I made her up." I could barely look Chloe in the eye. "I didn't want you to think I was all rubbish and lonely," I admitted.

To my embarrassment Chloe didn't even look surprised.

"I did kind of wonder," she said.

"You did?!"

She shrugged. "There was a clue," she said. "Doesn't matter now. I just don't understand why you lied! Why, Molly?"

"I suppose I was a bit ..." I didn't want to say
the word.

Unfortunately Notes was scribbling it all over
one of the toilet doors so there wasn't really any
escaping it.

Jealousings!!!

"A bit ... jealous," I said. "Jealous of you and
your new friends getting to hang out and do cool
stuff, while I'm just stuck at boring Dungfields.
And I'm jealous of Daffodil."

"Daffodil?!" said Chloe.

I sighed. "Yeah, I know it's nuts. I don't even know her! But she's like ... like ...

the new Molly!"

Something about the way I said it, all spluttery and pathetic, made me laugh. I tried not to, but *the new Molly* ... it just sounded so ridiculous! And then Chloe got the giggles too, and we both just stood there by the sinks, laughing so hard we could barely breathe.

Then when we finally stopped, Chloe said something I really needed to hear. "She's so not the new Molly, you absolute doughnut," she said. "You'll always be my best friend. I thought you knew that!"

Then we hugged.

"Sorry," I said.

"Me too," she said.

Why was *she* sorry, I wondered? Then I noticed Chloe was looking over *my* shoulder this time, at something Notes was now writing on the mirror.

"Is ... is everything OK?" I asked.

Chloe's bottom lip had begun to quiver.

"Kind of," she said. "OK-ish. It's just I didn't tell you the whole truth about everything. I sort of didn't want you to worry. And I sort of didn't want to think about how I was feeling."

Oh no. The thought of Chloe being upset made my bottom lip quiver too.

"What's wrong?" I said.

"Well, nothing really," she said. "But, also,

EVERYTHING!"

And then a whole bunch of stuff just poured out of her. "I'm still getting to know everyone and I'm always so worried about saying the

wrong thing or doing something silly. Because if they decide they don't like me I will literally have NO FRIENDS. And I keep getting things wrong in Maths because my class is doing stuff I've not done before. And I miss Mr Stilton!"

She laughed then, seeing my gaping mouth. "I know!" she giggled. "I do, though! I always kind of knew what to expect with old cheesy, but I don't really know Miss Wendle yet. Everything's new. Everything's different."

I didn't know what to say.

Eventually I did speak, though. "I've been horrendous," I said.

Chloe half smiled. "Well, maybe a little bit."

"I'm so sorry," I said. "Are you going to be OK at Lady Juniper's?"

Chloe shrugged. "Yeah," she said. "I'll be OK. Everyone really is friendly. It's just not the same. And I miss you, Molly. So please keep writing your notes. I need them."

All around the room, Notes had drawn smiles and sunshine and rainbows. I got the feeling she was maybe a little bit happy.

Luckily she'd used her magic pencil that only friendlings can see, because right at that moment the door swung open.

In came Mia and Grace. I noticed Alfie and
Marvin hopping up and down just outside too.
I gave them a wave and they did that scoopy
hurry-up thing with their hands.

What was the hurry?

"Mr Stilton said we could come and get you!
Everything sorted?" asked Grace.

I smiled at Chloe. She smiled back.

"Sorted," we said.

"Good," said Mia, "because it's getting exciting
out there! There's just two kids left, this boy from

St Humble's and Emily!"

"Emily?!" I said.

"Let's go!" said Chloe.

We snuck back in as quietly as possible
and sat on the back row of chairs.

On stage, a few girls (Daffodil included) waved
at Chloe from the bench. And get this ... I was
glad! There literally wasn't even one tiny smidge
of jealousy in me. I didn't even want to flick
Daffodil on the nose for saying I was horrendous
any more (or maybe just a tiny bit).

The boy from St Humble's had just finished
spelling "axolotyl" (one of my words!!) and from all
the clapping I guessed he'd got it right.

Then it was Emily's turn again.

"Emily," said the clipboard lady, **"spell
'UNEASINESS.'"**

Emily didn't even hesitate. "Uneasiness ...

Clipboard lady nodded, followed by more
clapping.

Then she said to the boy from St Humble's,
"Archie, spell 'DISAPPOINTMENT."

And he went ...

which is wrong, so he was out!
But Emily hadn't won yet. To win she had to get
her word right. If she got it wrong, it would be a
tie.

We all held our breath, waiting for the word.

Please, I thought, *please let it be one she knows! She deserves this and she's soooo close!*

"Emily, for a chance to win, spell 'SAPPHIRE.'"

And then Emily went ...

S-A-P-P-H-I-R-E

so of course I thought she'd messed up, because that spelling makes no sense AT ALL.

"Oh no!" I whispered to Chloe.

Chloe just smirked.

Then everyone started clapping and cheering.

"What's going on?" I said, but then I realised Emily must have spelled it right after all. I was the one who'd been spelling it wrong. And THAT was how Chloe guessed my friend Saffire wasn't really real!

CHAPTER ELEVEN

The clipboard lady gave Emily a bit of paper and a handshake, and everyone clapped again. Then someone with a camera **bigger than my head** took a photo of Emily holding the bit of paper, and everyone clapped a third time. She was like a proper superstar and I was super proud of her.

Eventually we had to get back into our school groups and I had to say goodbye to Chloe.

I watched as she caught up with her other friends. Daffodil linked arms with her, and they all laughed about something.

It was OK, though. I'd got over the whole jealousy thing and I honestly did want Chloe to fit in at her new school. Plus, we'd promised to write WAY more often.

(We also promised to be MUCH more careful about sending Notes out in the rain. That was just far too scary for words.)

Most of us Dungfields kids were a bit bouncy by the time we got back on the coach. The boys

from Mrs Banton's were still a bit sulky but the
rest of us were all:

WooooHOOOO!

Marvin was kapowing all over the place. Alfie
and Grace kept high-fiving. Mia kept making
funny little *squeeeeeeeeeeeeeee* noises.
Even Mr Stilton was smiling.

I had to smile too.

Notes and Captain Purrkins were happily
curled up, dozing in my lap. Notes still clutched
her magic pencil. Every so often she sleep-wrote
random stuff on my trousers.

I figured she was
celebrating in her
dreams.

There was plenty
to celebrate!

The **Chloe-Molly** team
was back together. Plus, Emily had totally rocked
the inter-school thingy. Everything was just good,
good, goooooooooood.

That's when I noticed that Emily was a bit quiet.

She was sitting next to me, and she wasn't miserable. It was nothing that dramatic. But she wasn't all **fizzy-HAPPY-hyper** like the rest of us either.

"You were so amazing back there," I said.

"Thanks," she said. Then she did one of those smiles people do when they're not actually happy.

FAKE SMILE

sad eyebrows

serious eyes

REAL SMILE

high-up eyebrows!

sparkly eyes

It wasn't the kind of real smile you'd expect to see on an inter-whatsit champion, that's for sure.

"What's up?" I said.

She didn't answer at first. She just sighed and looked away. But then she probably realised I wasn't going to leave her alone until she told me.

"It's nothing. I was just hoping my mum and dad would come. They said they'd try," she mumbled.

"Oh," I said. I'd been so relieved my own parents weren't there. But maybe if I'd been a half-decent speller ... "Yeah, it's a shame they couldn't make it. I bet they really wanted to.

At least *we* were there. Your friends," I said, hoping that would make her feel better.

because now Emily stopped even trying to act happy. She just kind of sighed and stared at her hands.

"What's wrong?!" I said.

She turned to me and looked me straight in the eye. "I don't have friends, Molly. Everyone's here because they like you, not me."

"But ... but ... but we're friends! You and me. I mean, I know we don't always agree about everything ... and sometimes we're just very ...

different ... but ..." Urgh, why was this was so

hard?

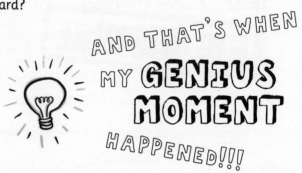

AND THAT'S WHEN MY **GENIUS MOMENT** HAPPENED!!!

The sun beamed through the minibus window.

A rainbow arched across the sky. I thought about

Chloe, I thought about all her new friends, I

thought about my friends. And I thought about

... maths. That's right. You heard me. **Maths.**

Wonderful, mathsy, mathematical maths!

"TESSELLATiNG SHAPES!!!" I yelled at
Emily, startling Notes and Captain Purrkins (oops).

"Err ...?!" said Emily, looking slightly scared.

"We're not all tessellating shapes!" I said
(again, slightly loud.)

By now all the kapowing, high-fiving and
squeeeing had stopped. Everyone was leaning in
and listening.

"No, Molly. No, we're not. We're human
beings. Are you feeling all right?"

I had to explain my genius thinking quickly or everyone would think I was crazy.

"I'm fine – just listen a moment," I said. "So, me and Chloe are best friends, right, because we have loads in common. We fit together from pretty much every single angle. We tessellate! Kind of ..."

Emily said nothing but kept listening.

I carried on ... "And you and me – actually all of us lot – we don't tessellate! We fit together from some angles but not all angles. And that just means you need more people to fit all the angles. See?!"

She didn't look like she saw.

"Thanks for trying," she sighed.

I could see Marvin bopping around on his seat, doing what I *think* was some kind of angle-dance.

Next to him, Alfie nodded like he kind of got it. In the seat ahead Mia and Grace started chatting about something totally different.

But Notes got it. My clever little scribble witch. She got it completely.

CHAPTER TWELVE

We were back at school in time for lunch. I ate
with Grace and Alfie, then did handstands for
a while with Mia and Marvin. I called Emily
over, but she didn't want to join in. She still only
looked half happy, even though everyone was
telling her well done.

KAPOW!

YAY!

AMAZING

Well done!

You ro

Nice one!

Go Emily!

In English we had to write persuasive letters.
We had to think about something we wanted, or
didn't want, or whatever, and we had to write
to someone about it. Like, you could write to
the government to convince them to give schools
more pencil sharpeners, or you could write to

your favourite pop star to convince them to visit Bogdale.

But those examples are a bit rubbish. My idea was way better – I was going to write to Mr Stilton. But first I was going to need Notes' super-speedy writing powers to help me. Because I also needed to write to **EVERYONE ELSE** in our class!!

This was my letter to the kids:

Hi,

I am writing to bring your attention to a mega-important matter. Emily. Emily is the matter because Emily matters!

As you know, Emily won the Inter-School Spelling Championship today, because she is super smart and tries **really** hard. So Emily basically rocks.

She deserves to be soooooo happy right now, but she JUST ISN'T. She's all down in the dumps because her mum and dad weren't there to see her big win. And we can't fix that. But we can show her that we all care and that we're all her friends.

So this is what you need to do: think of one thing you like about Emily and write it on a bit of paper.

I'll collect all the bits together ready for stage two of the plan (stage two is secret and exciting ... stay tuned!).

Pleeeeeease do this.

Thank you!

From **Molly**

Notes had been reading the whole time I was writing, and, when I finished, she leapt up and hugged my nose. Then she picked up her magic pencil and scrawled across the table ...

Molly is wondrous-good friendling!!!!

Then Notes – my wonderful scribble witch – copied it out eight times so that there was a letter for each table. And she sneakily delivered it (I had to hope no one would notice).

Next, I wrote to Mr Stilton.

Dear Mr Stilton,

Today, Emily is our champion.

This is a big deal for Dungfields! Let's face it, we never win sports stuff, plus my dad says test results are rubbish here. So we should celebrate. And how should we celebrate?

With a proper award ~~serramony~~ ~~ceramony~~ ceremony!!!!

Let's show her how much we care and how impressed we are and stuff!

We could make paper chains from scrap paper. And maybe a medal if there's some of that gold card left over from Christmas? I'm not sure what else.

It wouldn't need to be a BIG ceremony, just something fun to end the day with.

Say yes.

Yours sincerely,

Molly

P.S. I bet you're glad we beat Mrs Banton's class too. So that's another reason to celebrate.

That last bit is true. Mr Stilton and Mrs
Banton annoy each other — you can just tell.

Then I took my open book over to Mr Stilton.

"Oh!" he said, clearly surprised by my
keenness. "Put it on my desk, next to the pile."

"I can't," I said.

"Why can't you?"

"Because it's urgent. Please can you read it
right now?" I said.

He shook his head but took it and read it

anyway, which was confusing.

When he finished he shook his head again.
"I'm sorry," he said. "It's a kind thought, but
there's no gold card left and there's no time to
make scrap-paper chains."

"Oh," I said.

I shouldn't have been surprised. Mr Stilton
doesn't like fun. Still, my letter was really
persuasive. So I'd kind of persuaded myself he'd
say "yes".

"I really am sorry,
Molly," he said.

"OK," I said (it was SO NOT OK!!!) and I moped my way back to my seat.

Notes was doing magic doodling on the table when I got there.

She looked up with a big grin on her face, then stopped grinning when she saw me.

I nodded.

Notes' little eyes narrowed in concentration.

Notes and Captain Purrkins will fix its!

She wrote quickly, even by her crazy-quick
standards, then she grabbed Captain Purrkins,
jumped on her pencil and zoomed off over my
head.

I would have looked to see where she was
headed, but right at that moment I heard a
SNIFF from Emily.

I grabbed my notepad ...

Seconds later I got this ...

... followed by another **SNIFF** and a fairly loud

SOB.

Oh.

"Emily," I whispered, "do you want a hug?"

Emily isn't a huggy kind of person, but I didn't know what to write or what to say, so a hug was all I could offer.

She shrugged. "Maybe." (I guessed this actually meant yes.)

So I lunged towards her and squished her shoulders into a massive cuddle.

And just when I was about to let go Marvin leaned over and joined in, yelling, "Quick! Fist pump for the Spelling Queen!"

Which sent me and Emily into mega-giggles.

Mr Stilton was now at his desk marking books. Everyone was either working or chatting. So for ages no one noticed what had happened. Including me.

But when Marvin eventually unhugged us we looked around the room and saw ...

"Who did this?" gasped Emily.

"KAPOW!" yelled Marvin.

By now everyone was starting to notice. Mustafa shouted **"Whoa!"**, Mia yelped in surprise, Dylan B. called out, **"GOOD ONE, MOLLY!"** They all thought I'd done it. Including Mr Stilton.

"That was quick work, Molly!" he said. "How did you ... but what about ... and all the ... huh?!?"

"I ... I had a bit of help," I said.

I gulped and looked at Emily. "I can't explain," I whispered, "but trust me, it's all good."

She nodded, eyes beyond wide.

"Well," said Mr Stilton, still struggling to understand what had happened, "I suppose Emily should come to the front for the, er, award ceremony. And, er, Molly ... do you want to say a few words?"

I nodded. I did want to. But also I didn't want it to be just me saying stuff.

"Has any one got any, er, *bits of paper* for me?" I asked.

I hoped maybe a few people would say yes. But it was so much better than that.

CHAPTER THIRTEEN

Every single kid in our class had written something for Emily.

I collected all the bits of paper in this fantabulous trophy that Notes and Captain Purrkins had clearly made together.

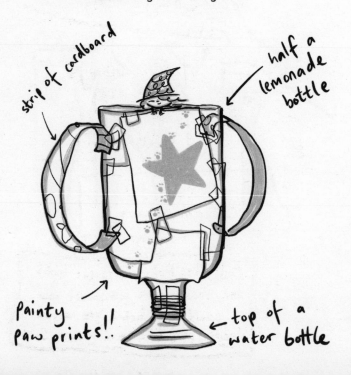

strip of cardboard

half a lemonade bottle

painty paw prints!!

top of a water bottle

Then I handed it over to Emily and told her
we were all proud to know her.

She read the notes and cried, actually cried.
But it was happy crying, I think.

These are my top ten things people wrote
about Emily:

10. Emily has neat hair

9. She always takes my problems seriously.

8. Emily knows lots of clever things.

7. Emily likes books and I like books and books make you smart and smartness helps you write loads just like I'm doing now. See?

6.

Emily loves pencil toppers.
SO DO I!!

↖ my one!

5.

Emily is cind wen
I am wurried or
sad.

4.

Emily can write
nice like teachers
write nice.

3.

One time when I was hit in
the head with a basketball
Emily took me to the
first aid room.

2.

Emily knows all our
birthdays.

1.

Emily can say
ABRACADABRA backwards
(she doesn't see the point though)

↖ Arbadacarba!

Then Mr Stilton put the paper crown on Emily's head, and everyone clapped and cheered.

And to top it off, while I'd been talking, Mia had made me this medal ...

The whole thing was the BEST scrap-paper, junk-modelling extravaganza EVER.

runner up

Chloe,

Notes really saved the day AGAIN. She did this amazing award ceremony for Emily. It was nuts. Everything was made of scrap, but it was still brilliant. Mia even made this runner-up thingy out of paper clips.

Anyway, I really AM sorry about the whole jealousy thing. I promise to be less like this

And more like this

Jealous-Crazy-
Molly-monster

Wise and cool and
mostly normal

Your new friends are going to love you sooooo much when they get to know you.

And it doesn't matter if you don't have EVERYTHING in common with EVERYONE as long as you've got something in common with lots of someones.

We're both just super lucky because we ~~tesserlate tessalate~~ tessellate. Or something.

Love you, bestie!

From Molly xxxx

P.S. Please tell Daffodil I'm not normally like that.

P.P.S. Sending Daffodil the runner-up thing as an extra sorry.

P.P.P.S. Actually, I can't think of anything else. That's all for now!

P.P.P.P.S. Write back soon! xxx

Read on for more
SCRiBBLE WiTCH
adventures in book 3:

Paper friends

Hey,

So much is happening at school!
There's a new girl called Amelie
who's like some kind of genius AND
we're off on a school trip to learn
about all things ancient Egypt.
Plus, there's a mysterious object
buried in the playground and
we're dying to dig it up. Fancy
coming along for the ride?

Molly x

Halloo friendlings,
Is me, Notes, secret paper witchy.
I is helping Molly with super
important ~~questings~~ questions like
where dids Egypters get
toilet rolls for mummy wrappings
and why is shapes pyramids
not cones? Maybeez I find
out on school trip.
I wonder if ancient Egypters
hads paper witchy friendlings too...
Byezees for now!
  Notes
      x